When I Feel Scared

WRITTEN BY

Cornelia Maude Spelman

ILLUSTRATED BY

Kathy Parkinson

www.av2books.com

Your AV² Media Enhanced book gives you a fiction readalong online. Log on to www.av2books.com and enter the unique book code from this page to use your readalong.

AV² Readalong Navigation

HIGHLIGHTED TEXT   HOME 🏠   CLOSE ⊗

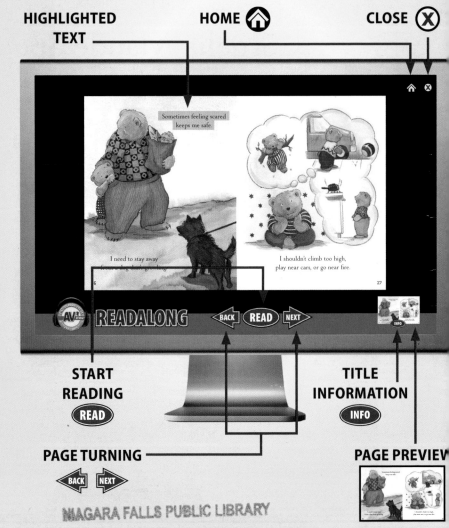

START READING
READ

PAGE TURNING
BACK NEXT

TITLE INFORMATION
INFO

PAGE PREVIEW

Go to **www.av2books.com**, and enter this book's unique code.

BOOK CODE

M429632

AV² by Weigl brings you media enhanced books that support active learning.

First Published by

ALBERT WHITMAN & COMPANY
Publishing children's books since 1919

Published by AV² by Weigl
350 5ᵗʰ Avenue, 59ᵗʰ Floor New York, NY 10118
Copyright ©2013 AV² by Weigl
Printed in the United States of America in North Mankato, Minnesota
1 2 3 4 5 6 7 8 9 0 16 15 14 13 12

Text copyright © 2002 by Cornelia Maude Spelman.
Illustrations copyright © 2002 by Kathy Parkinson.
Published in 2002 by Albert Whitman & Company.

052012
WEP160512

Library of Congress Cataloging-in-Publication Data

Spelman, Cornelia.
 When I feel scared / written by Cornelia Maude Spelman ; illustrated by Kathy Parkinson.
    p. cm.
 Summary: A young bear describes situations that bring about fear, how it feels to be scared, and what can make things better.
 ISBN 978-1-61913-141-5 (hardcover : alk. paper)
 [1. Fear--Fiction. 2. Bears--Fiction.] I. Parkinson, Kathy, ill. II. Title.
 PZ7.S74727Wj 2012
 [E]--dc23
                                            2012021717

For all our children. — C. M. S.
For the Andersons, especially Reece and Etamo,
with love and every best wish. — K. P.

Note to Parents and Teachers

While there are times children need to tolerate their fright in order to learn from new situations, it isn't helpful to minimize or deny their fear. We may believe we're reassuring when we say, "That's nothing to be afraid of!" but this response can, in fact, hurt children by making them feel ashamed of an emotion that is both common and unavoidable.

For healthy development, children need to be able to identify their feelings and to receive acknowledgment, understanding, and comfort when they convey these feelings to adults. The child whose feeling is ignored or denied or who is made to feel embarrassed is left alone with an upsetting emotion and does not learn to seek help when needed.

Instead of downplaying children's fear, we need to acknowledge it and then show them how to manage it. Management will depend on the situation. Sometimes fear is appropriate, and actions based on fear keep children safe (staying away from a growling dog). Sometimes fear is unfounded, and we can help a child discover this by experiencing the fearful situation together (looking under the bed to see what's there; taking a pleasant walk in the dark). Sometimes fear must be tolerated (as in getting a shot), but we can stay in close physical and emotional contact with children and thus help them bear it ("I am right here with you").

We want our children to know that we will be attentive to all of their feelings—positive or negative; that all of the human family—children and adults—experience such feelings; and that we know how to deal with unpleasant emotions. We want to build our children's confidence in their coping ability, so that they will be able to say, "When I feel scared, I know what to do!"

Cornelia Maude Spelman, A.C.S.W., L.C.S.W.

4

Sometimes I feel scared.

I feel scared when there's a big, loud noise
or when I have a bad dream

or when my mother goes away.

When I think I could get hurt, I feel scared.

Sometimes I just feel scared
and I don't know why!

Scared is a cold, tight feeling.

When I feel scared,
I cry.

I want to run away,
or hide.

I want someone
to hold me.

I want to stop
feeling scared!

Everyone's scared sometimes, even grownups.
It's not being a baby to be scared.

When I feel scared, I can do some things to feel better
I can tell someone that I'm scared.

I can ask to be held. It helps to be held,
and to talk about what scares me.

13

I can cuddle with someone, with my
blanket or stuffed animal,

get in a cozy place, or look at
my favorite book.

Sometimes feeling scared
keeps me safe.

I need to stay away
from a dog that's growling.

I shouldn't climb too high,
play near cars, or go near fire.

Other times I don't need to be scared. We can look under the bed to see what's there.

I can learn that the dark can be nice.

I can pet a friendly dog
when its owner says I can.

I see that when my mother goes away,
she comes back again.

21

When I feel scared,
I can talk about it.

I can have someone
hold me.

I can cuddle with
my blanket or toy,

or find a cozy place.

I can find out that some things
aren't really scary.

When I feel scared, I know what to do!